The Dust Under
Mrs. Merriweather's Bed

The Dust Under Mrs. Merriweather's Bed

Susan Grohmann

WHISPERING COYOTE PRESS, INC.
BOSTON

Published by Whispering Coyote Press, Inc.
480 Newbury Street, Suite 104, Danvers, MA 01923
Copyright © 1994 by Susan Grohmann
All rights reserved including the right of reproduction in whole or in part in any form.
Printed in Singapore by Toppan Printing Company
Book production and design by Our House

Library of Congress Cataloging-in-Publication Data

Grohmann, Susan, 1948-
The dust under Mrs Merriweather's bed / story and pictures by Susan Grohmann.
  p.   cm.
Summary: As tidy Mrs. Merriweather, who lives in the sky, cleans her house and waters her garden, Kenny, who lives on earth, watches the consequent changes in the sky and in the weather.
ISBN 1-879085-82-8 : $14.95
[1. Weather--Fiction.] I. Title.
PZ7.G89257Du 1993

[E]-dc20

93-21804
CIP
AC

To my Parents

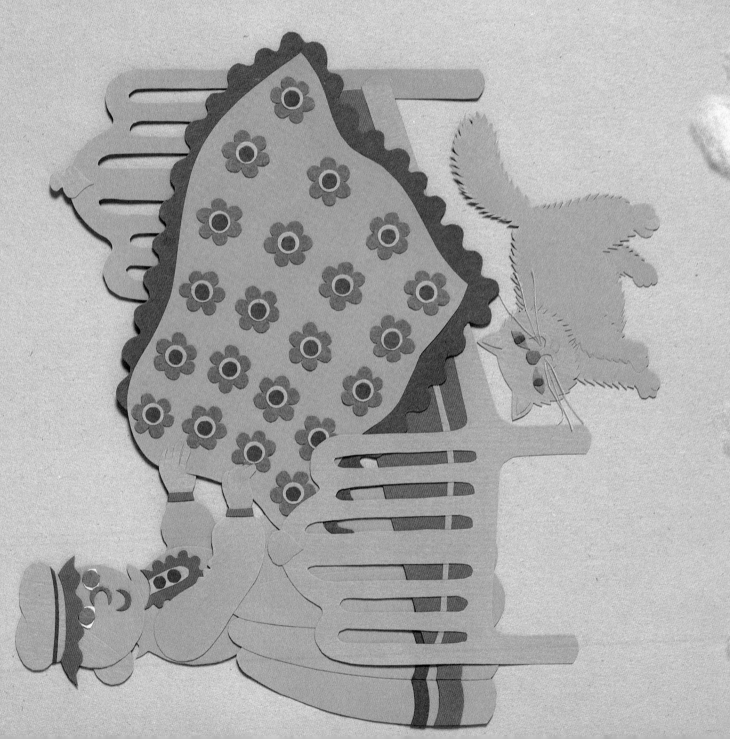

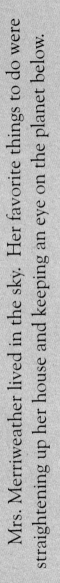

Mrs. Merriweather lived in the sky. Her favorite things to do were straightening up her house and keeping an eye on the planet below.

Down on earth, Kenny lived with his family. His favorite things to do were lying in the grass and watching the clouds above.

"Ah, time to relax," sighed Mrs. Merriweather. "I think I'll work on my embroidery." Mrs. Merriweather turned on a bright lamp so she could pick out just the right colors of thread and not miss a single tiny stitch.

"Ah, time for fun at the beach," said Kenny. "I think I'll build a sand castle."
Kenny loved to explore and dig in the sand.

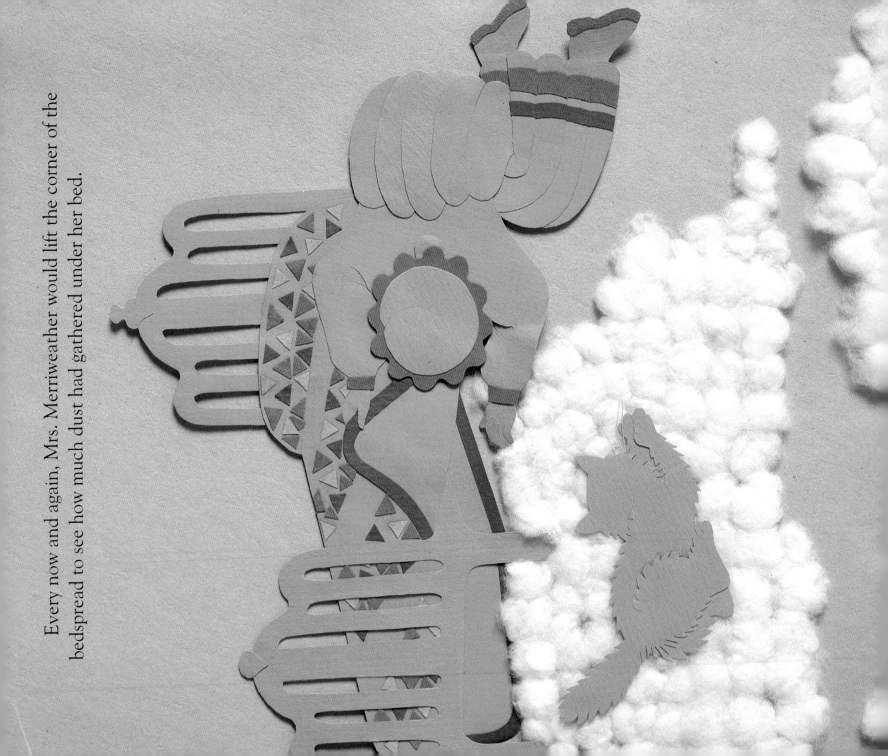

Every now and again, Mrs. Merriweather would lift the corner of the bedspread to see how much dust had gathered under her bed.

And every now and again, Kenny would look at the corner of the sky and consider the clouds.

If Mrs. Merriweather found a lot of dust, she would plug in her vacuum cleaner and run it under her bed.

When the sky was clear, Kenny would wonder where the clouds had raced off to in such a hurry and when they would return.

One day when Mrs. Merriweather plugged in her vacuum cleaner, nothing happened. "Oh, dear," she said, "it's broken. I must have it repaired." In the meantime, she used a broom to sweep the dust away. The broom didn't work as well as the vacuum cleaner—a few puffs of dust were left behind.

And that same day, Kenny was delighted when he looked up at the sky. "Oh, my," he said, "it's very cloudy today. Maybe it will rain later." But as he watched, the clouds began to break up and drift away. They were finally gone—almost.

It was summer, and Mrs. Merriweather went away on vacation for two weeks. When she returned home, she saw that the dust had piled up high under her bed. It was very dirty. "My broom will never do the job this time," she said. Mrs. Merriweather pushed the bed aside and used the garden hose to wash the dust away.

When Kenny returned home from two weeks at summer camp, he saw that the sky was full of heavy clouds. It was very dark. Kenny felt cool drops on his skin and was soon dancing in a refreshing afternoon rain.

One glorious fall afternoon, Mrs. Merriweather noticed that the bathroom smelled musty. It needed a good airing out. Mrs. Merriweather opened the window and switched on her fan.

Down below, Kenny was out riding his bicycle after school. As he pedaled along, the wind suddenly kicked up. Brilliantly colored autumn leaves shook from the trees and swirled all around him.

The cool air of fall turned into the frigid air of winter. There were still plenty of indoor chores for Mrs. Merriweather to do. "Look out Kitty!" cried Mrs. Merriweather. "Oh, my! Now I must get my broom and sweep up this mess!"

Kenny woke up and ran to his bedroom window. "Oh boy, it's snowing!" laughed Kenny. He hurried to put on his boots and mittens and ran outside to play.

One warm spring day Mrs. Merriweather was outside tending her vegetable garden. She sprinkled the thirsty plants with her watering can before going back indoors.

Down on the earth below, Kenny was planting flowers in his garden. Suddenly a warm spring rain began to fall. Kenny smiled up at the sky as he patted the moist soil around his new plants.

Up in the sky, Mrs. Merriweather was always content as long as she was busy.

And on the planet below, Kenny was always curious and happy, gazing up at the ever-changing sky.